Sorry!

Norbert Landa Tim Warnes

LITTLE TIGER PRESS
London

Bear and Rabbit were the best friends you can imagine.

They lived in their Bear-Rabbit house.

They cooked their Bear-Rabbit meals
in their Bear-Rabbit kitchen.

Rabbit was better at frying mushrooms.
Bear was perfect at making honey-cakes.

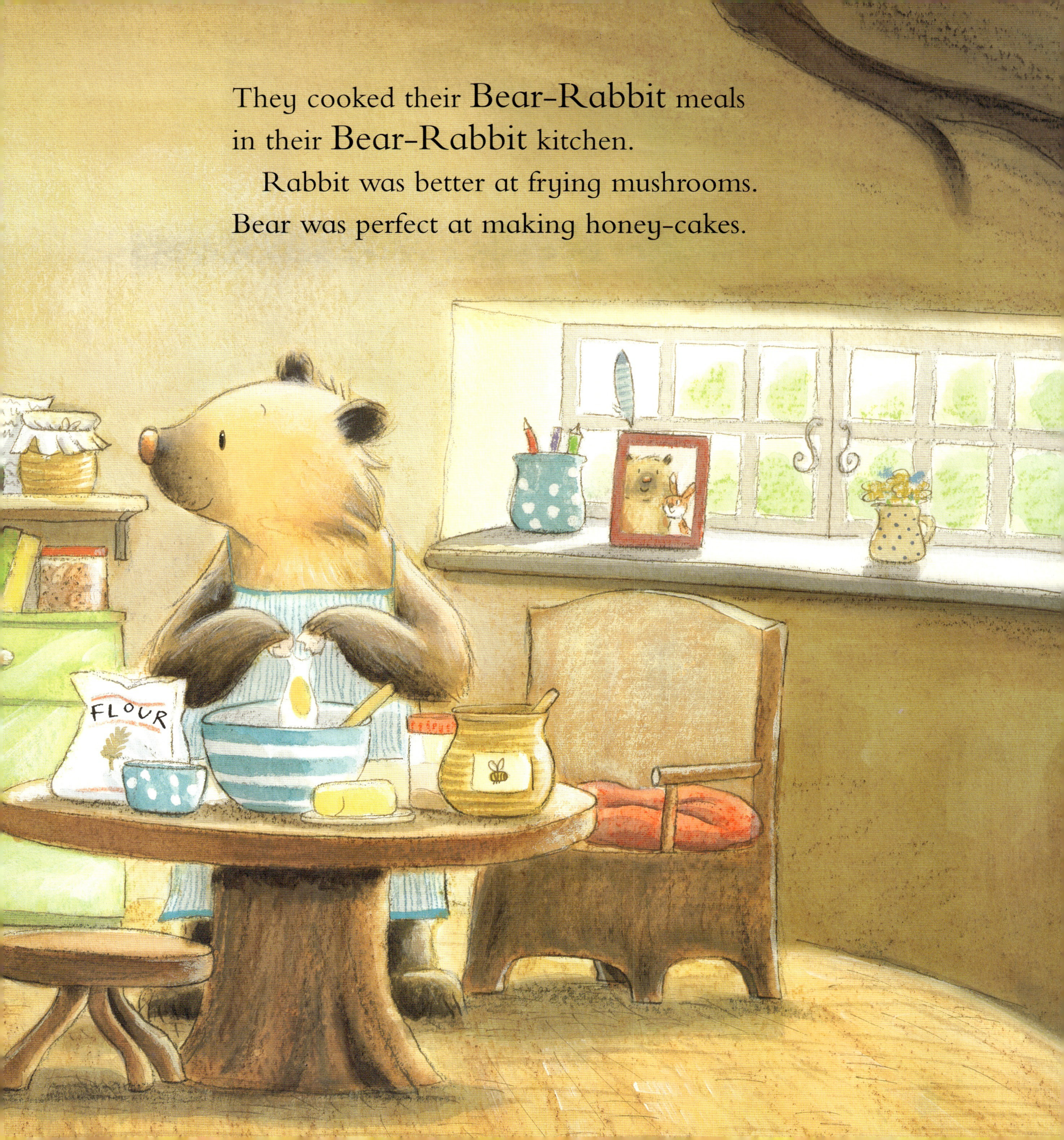

At night they slept in their Bear-Rabbit bunk bed. Rabbit slept below. Bear slept above, because he was better at climbing.

In summer they lived in their tree house.
Rabbit told stories to Bear, because he
was better at telling stories.

It was a wonderful feeling being a good
friend and having a good friend.

One summer morning, Rabbit saw something blinking and twinkling in the sun.

"Look, Bear!" he said. "What's that down there?"

Bear lowered Rabbit to
the ground in his basket and
climbed down.

Then they ran to look
for the strange thing.

Bear went right up close and looked into it. He had never seen a thing so shiny!

"Goodness," he said. "It's a picture of me! Look, Rabbit. What fluffy Bear ears I have!"

So Rabbit looked into the shiny thing.
"You're kidding," he said. "It's a picture of me!
My pretty, long ears, don't you see them?"

"You are completely wrong," said Bear, grabbing the shiny thing. "These are small and round and fluffy Bear ears. This is my picture!"

Rabbit grabbed

and Bear pulled and

Rabbit pushed

and Bear tugged.

And the two of them tore the shiny thing into two.

Then
they
both
stormed
off . . .

with
their
own
little
piece.

Oh, how mad Rabbit was! He strode back to Bear-Rabbit house and slammed the door.

Then he stuck the shiny thing to the wall, so he could look at his picture and proudly say,

"Wonderful, pretty, long ears!"

Then he went to bed. What else could
he do, alone in Bear-Rabbit house?

Meanwhile, angry Bear
climbed up the tree house
and stuck his piece to
the wall.

He sat down on
the bench, to
admire himself
and his round,
fluffy ears.

Then he looked down to Bear-Rabbit house.

"I could really do without *such a* friend,"

he grumbled.

Evening came and night came. But Rabbit could not sleep and he wasn't angry any more.

"How silly I was!" he sighed.

"How good it would be to have Bear here with me, so I could tell him a wonderful goodnight story."

Up in the tree house
Bear stared at the moon.
He was sad and he felt
lonely, just like Rabbit.

What can I do to make
Rabbit happy and be my
friend again? he thought.

Then Bear had an idea. He took his
little piece of the **shiny thing**
and climbed down the tree.
Quietly he padded to
Bear-Rabbit house.

But Rabbit was not in bed, either.
He was standing outside, holding in
his hand his own little piece.

When he saw Bear, Rabbit walked towards him and whispered, "Sorry, Bear. You can have my picture!"

"Oh no, I'm sorry!" Bear said and gave him his own.

But when they got into a huddle
and looked at the shiny things,
what did they see . . . ?

. . . a picture of both of them!

"That's just perfect!" said Bear and Rabbit happily.